Dear Parents:

Congratulations! Your child is taking the first steps on an exciting journey. The destination? Independent reading!

STEP INTO READING® will help your child get there. The program offers five steps to reading success. Each step includes fun stories and colorful art or photographs. In addition to original fiction and books with favorite characters, there are Step into Reading Non-Fiction Readers, Phonics Readers and Boxed Sets, Sticker Readers, and Comic Readers—a complete literacy program with something to interest every child.

Learning to Read, Step by Step!

Ready to Read   Preschool–Kindergarten
• big type and easy words • rhyme and rhythm • picture clues
For children who know the alphabet and are eager to begin reading.

Reading with Help   Preschool–Grade 1
• basic vocabulary • short sentences • simple stories
For children who recognize familiar words and sound out new words with help.

Reading on Your Own   Grades 1–3
• engaging characters • easy-to-follow plots • popular topics
For children who are ready to read on their own.

Reading Paragraphs   Grades 2–3
• challenging vocabulary • short paragraphs • exciting stories
For newly independent readers who read simple sentences with confidence.

Ready for Chapters   Grades 2–4
• chapters • longer paragraphs • full-color art
For children who want to take the plunge into chapter books but still like colorful pictures.

STEP INTO READING® is designed to give every child a successful reading experience. The grade levels are only guides; children will progress through the steps at their own speed, developing confidence in their reading.

Remember, a lifetime love of reading starts with a single step!

Step into Reading, Random House, and the Random House colophon are registered trademarks
of Penguin Random House LLC.

Visit us on the Web!
StepIntoReading.com
randomhousekids.com

Educators and librarians, for a variety of teaching tools, visit us at RHTeachersLibrarians.com

ISBN 978-0-7364-3803-2 (trade) — ISBN 978-0-7364-9017-7 (lib. bdg.)
ISBN 978-0-7364-3768-4 (ebook)

Printed in the United States of America   10 9 8 7 6 5 4 3 2 1

DISNEY · PIXAR

BRAVE

MERIDA
IS BRAVE

by Cherie Gosling

illustrated by the
Disney Storybook Art Team

Random House 🏠 New York

One day,
Merida's brothers want
to climb a cliff.
Merida laughs.

She tells them
it is too hard.

They will

climb anyway.

Hamish goes first.
His brothers give
him a boost.

Oh, no!

Hamish slips.

He needs help!

Harris finds

Merida.

Merida, Harris,
and Hubert
ride Angus
to the cliff.

They see Hamish.
They also see some
will o' the wisps.
Hamish is in danger!

Harris and Hubert
make a pile
of leaves.

Merida ties an arrow
to a rope.
She shoots the arrow
over a tree branch.

Hubert ties the rope
to Angus.

Angus walks
up a hill.
Hubert keeps
the rope tied.

Merida holds on.
The rope pulls her
up the cliff.

The will o' the wisps
make Hamish fall.
Merida reaches
for her brother.

She catches him!

The will o' the wisps

fly away.

Hamish hugs Merida.

The rope lowers

Merida and Hamish

to the ground.

Hamish lands
in the leaves.
He is safe!

Merida hugs
her brothers.
They worked together
to help Hamish.

She is proud of them.

She thanks Angus

for his help.

The boys say
they are as brave
as their sister.
Merida agrees!

They are safe and warm,
thanks to Cri-Kee
the lucky cricket!

24

Dear Parents:

Congratulations! Your child is taking the first steps on an exciting journey. The destination? Independent reading!

STEP INTO READING® will help your child get there. The program offers five steps to reading success. Each step includes fun stories and colorful art or photographs. In addition to original fiction and books with favorite characters, there are Step into Reading Non-Fiction Readers, Phonics Readers and Boxed Sets, Sticker Readers, and Comic Readers—a complete literacy program with something to interest every child.

Learning to Read, Step by Step!

Ready to Read   Preschool–Kindergarten
• big type and easy words • rhyme and rhythm • picture clues
For children who know the alphabet and are eager to begin reading.

Reading with Help   Preschool–Grade 1
• basic vocabulary • short sentences • simple stories
For children who recognize familiar words and sound out new words with help.

Reading on Your Own   Grades 1–3
• engaging characters • easy-to-follow plots • popular topics
For children who are ready to read on their own.

Reading Paragraphs   Grades 2–3
• challenging vocabulary • short paragraphs • exciting stories
For newly independent readers who read simple sentences with confidence.

Ready for Chapters   Grades 2–4
• chapters • longer paragraphs • full-color art
For children who want to take the plunge into chapter books but still like colorful pictures.

STEP INTO READING® is designed to give every child a successful reading experience. The grade levels are only guides; children will progress through the steps at their own speed, developing confidence in their reading.

Remember, a lifetime love of reading starts with a single step!

Step into Reading, Random House, and the Random House colophon are registered trademarks of Penguin Random House LLC.

Visit us on the Web!
StepIntoReading.com
randomhousekids.com

Educators and librarians, for a variety of teaching tools, visit us at RHTeachersLibrarians.com

ISBN 978-0-7364-3803-2 (trade) — ISBN 978-0-7364-9017-7 (lib. bdg.)
ISBN 978-0-7364-3768-4 (ebook)

Printed in the United States of America   10 9 8 7 6 5 4 3 2 1

Disney
PRINCESS

MULAN
IS LOYAL

by Cherie Gosling

illustrated by the
Disney Storybook Art Team

Random House 🏠 New York

It is snowing!
Mulan and her family
are at home.
Mulan washes dishes.

Fa Li sews.

Fa Zhou reads.

Oh, no!

Fa Zhou and Fa Li

have some bad luck.

Cri-Kee the lucky cricket
is gone!

Mulan looks for him.
He is not
in the house.
She looks outside.

She sees his footprints
in the snow!

Mulan finds Mushu.

She asks him

to help.

Mushu does not want
to go out in the snow.
But he agrees.

Mulan and Mushu
follow the trail.
Mushu sneezes.
The trail melts!

Mushu is worried.
He knows Cri-Kee
hates the cold.

Mulan and Mushu
try to find the trail.
It is cold.
It is snowy.

Clouds make it
hard to see.

Mushu has an idea.

He breathes a little fire.

Now Mulan can see.

She finds Cri-Kee's tracks!

They follow the trail
to a cave.

They dig out
the cave opening.

Cri-Kee is inside
with a little girl!

She was lost.

Cri-Kee found her

and kept her safe.

The friends warm up
by a fire.
Mulan thanks Cri-Kee
for helping the girl.

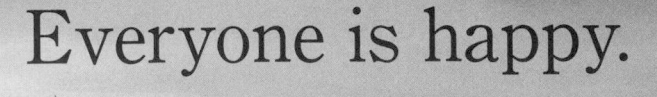

Everyone is happy.